# Welcome to
# Princess Friends
# Coloring and Activity Book

This book belongs to _____

 I am _____ years old

My favorite color is _____

Questions, comments or concerns, we would love to hear from you.
Contact us at: bluejewelbooks@gmail.com
Please help us grow our business by leaving an honest review of this book on Amazon. Thank you.

Published by Blue Jewel Books
Copyright © 2021

Blue Jewel Books

# Help the little princess get to the tower.

One item in each row is different from the others.
Find and circle it!

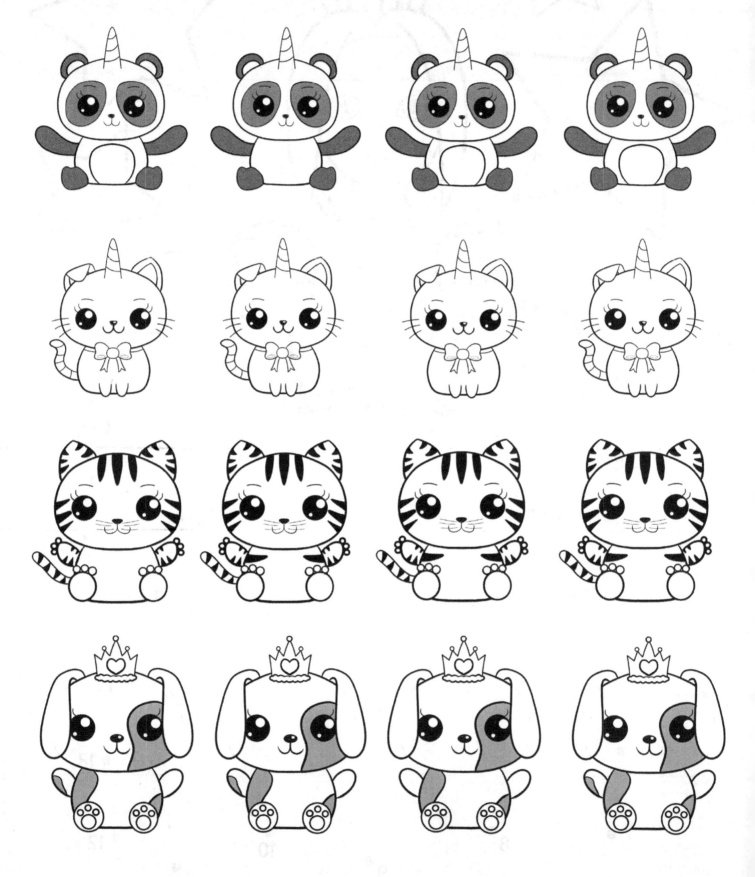

# Follow the trails! Which one takes the mermaid to the treasure chest?

# Help the pegasus get to the castle in the clouds

# Color by Number!
1 - Yellow   2 - Pink   3 - Orange
4 - Blue   5 - Green

# Help the fairy fly through the tree.

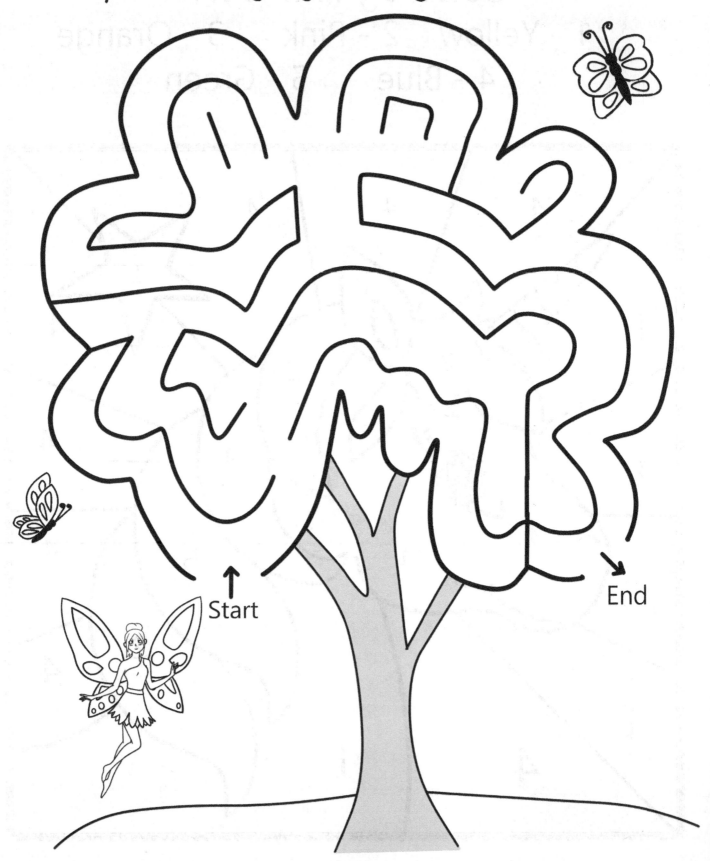

Start

End

# Trace over the letter outlines to complete the words.

CROWN

HEART

WAND

ROSE

# Help the baby Narwhal get to her mommy!

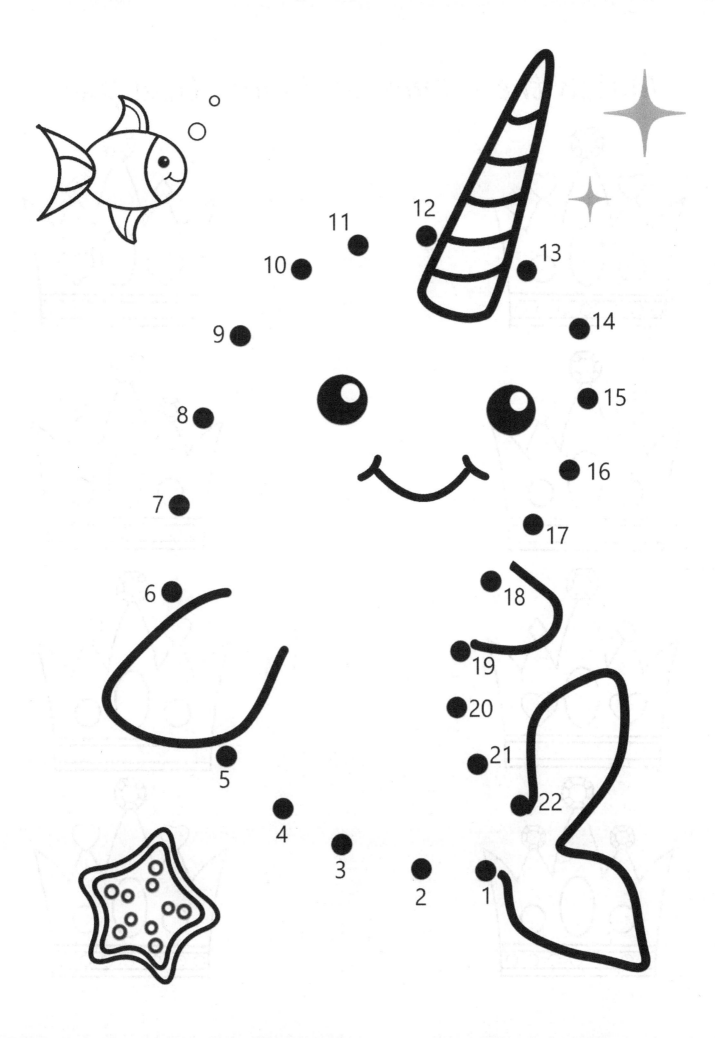

# Match the crown to its identical pair

# Draw a line to match the animals to their shadows.

# One item in each row is different from the others. Find and circle it!

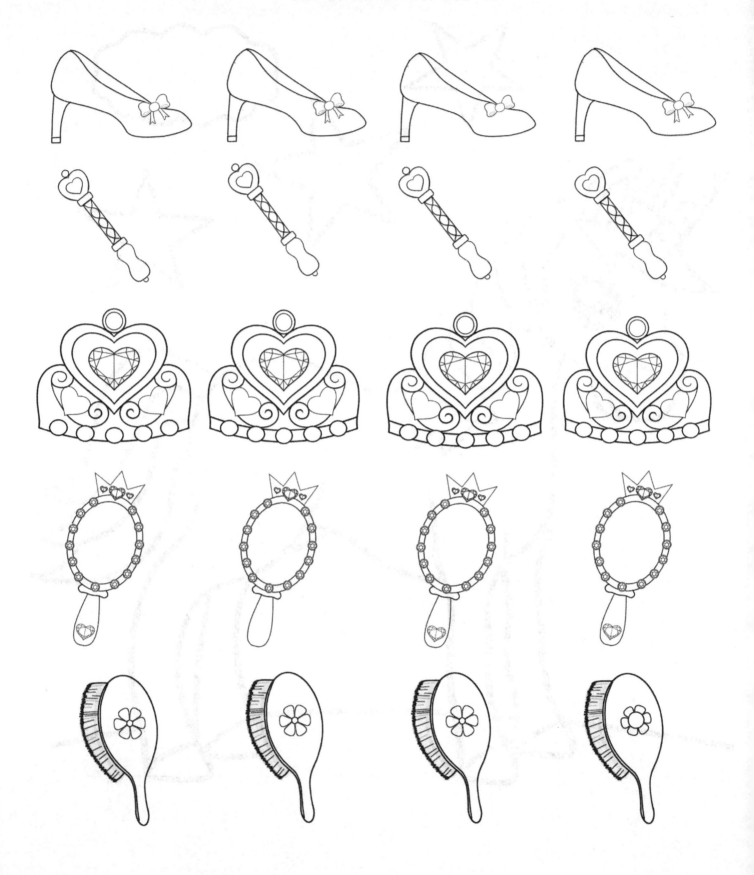

Can you find 6 hearts in this picture?
Then, color it in!

# Can you spot 8 differences between these pictures?

# Help the puppy find her lost crown

# Help the princess find her kitten.

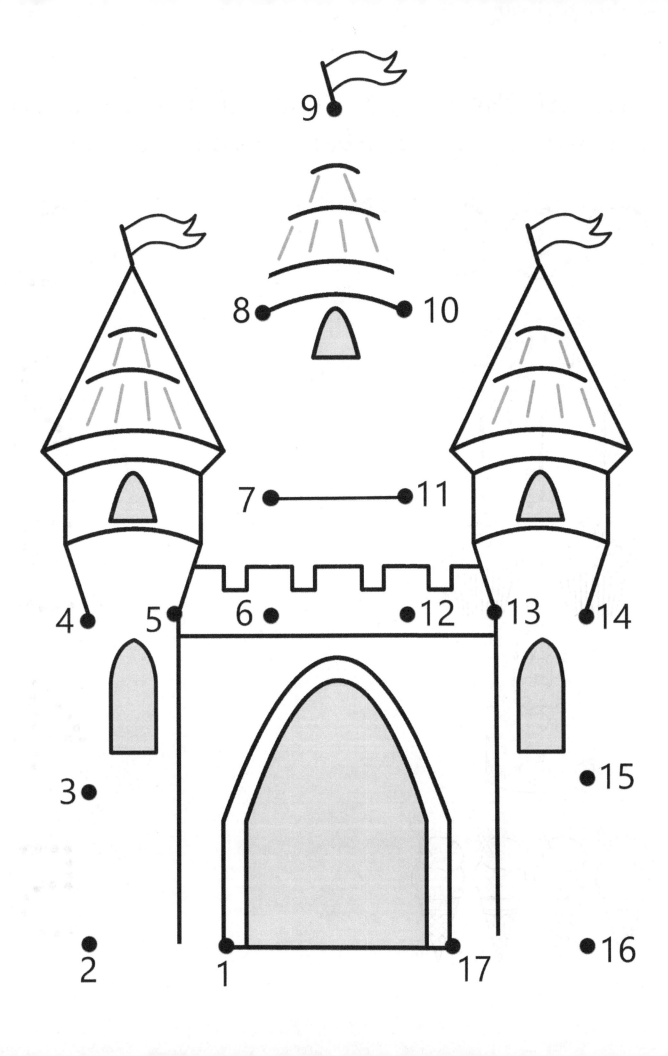

# Count the objects. Then draw a line to the matching number. Trace the numbers.

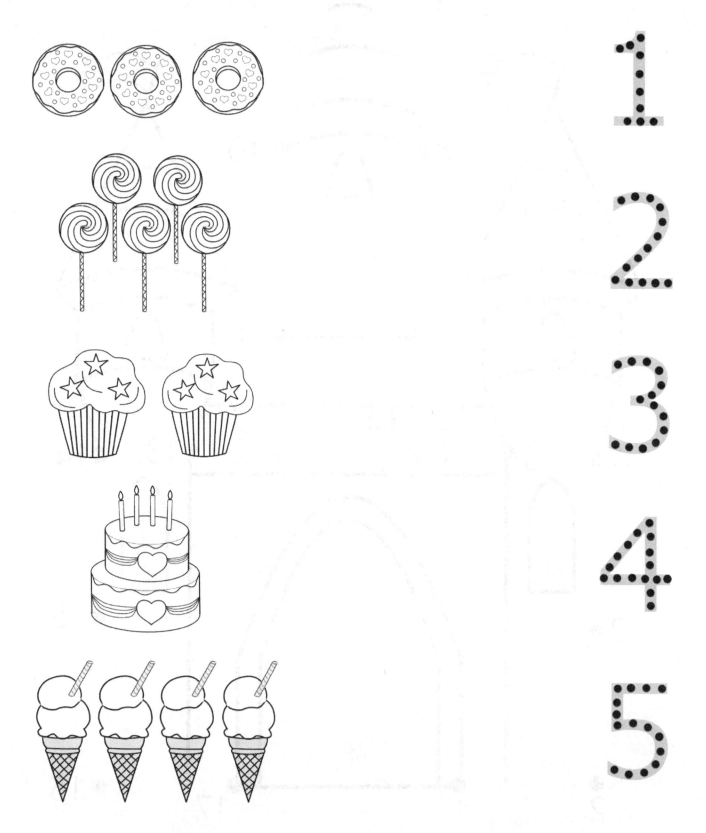

# Follow the path!
Help the mermaid get to her friend the jellyfish.

Start

End

Start

End

# Color by Number!
1 - Red    2 - Orange    3 - Yellow
4 - Green   5 - Blue    6 - Purple   7- Pink

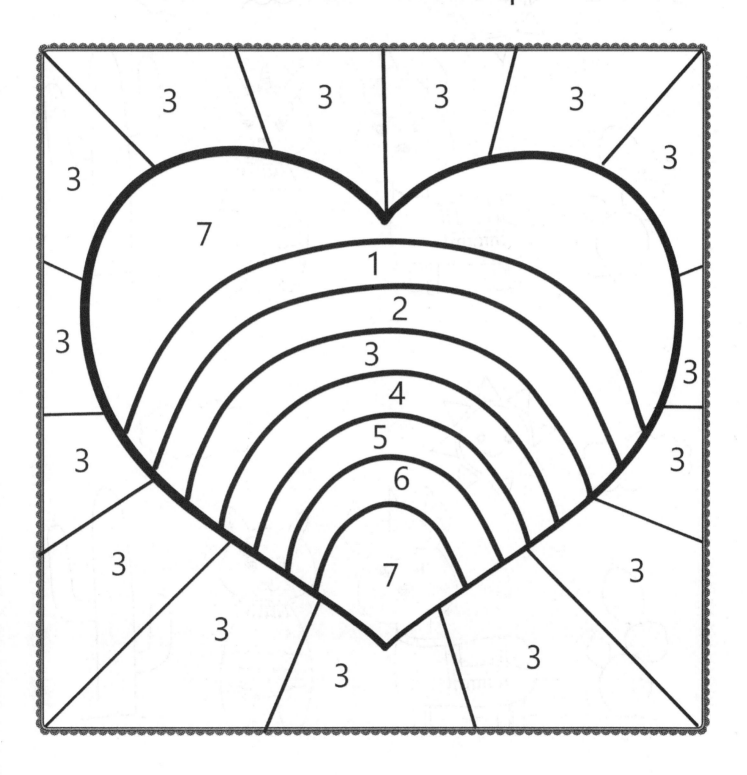

# Can you spot 6 differences between these pictures?

# Trace the flowers and stems, then color the picture!

Can you draw the horns on these animals?
Then color them in!

Search among the treasure for one jewel shaped like a rectangle , two jewels shaped like an oval, and three heart shaped jewels. Color the picture!

# Follow the trails! Which one takes the princess to her crown?

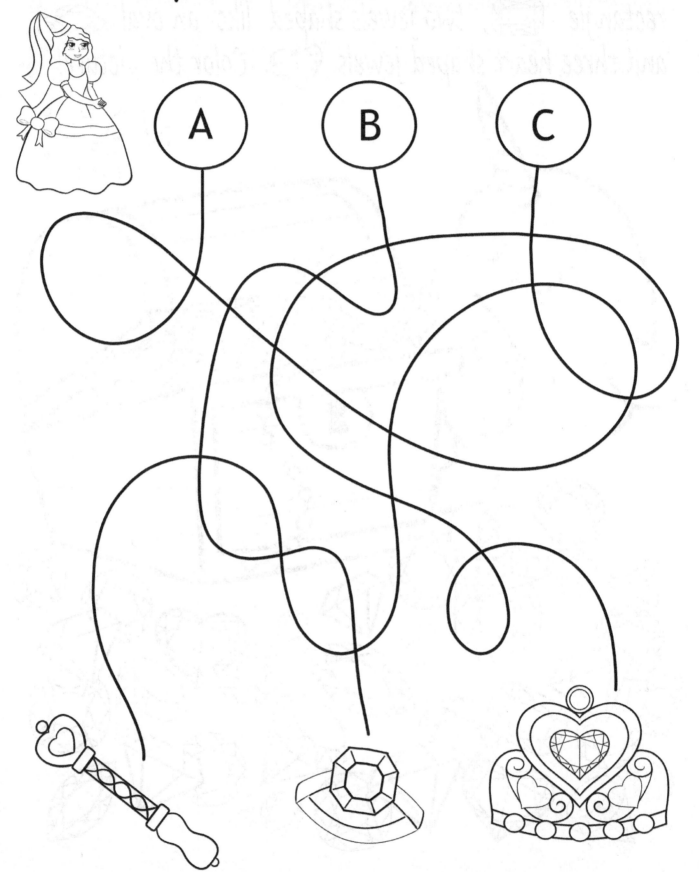

# Help the panda get to the cupcake!

# I Spy! Find and count these objects

3  7  2  5

4  2  3  3

Did you find all of these?

# Lollipop Maze

Start

End

# Find the popsicle that does not have a match, then color the picture!

# Help the fairy get to the flowers.

Start

End

Which path should the fairy take to spell the word FLOWER?

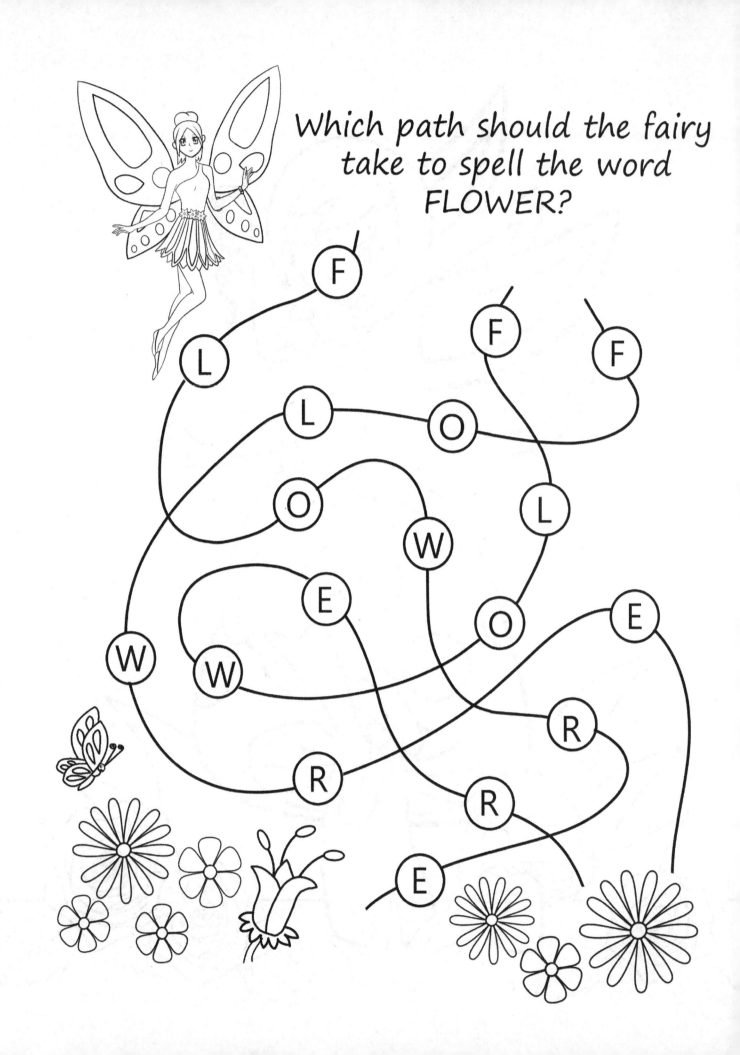

# Trace the lines to help the animals get to the flowers.

Complete these snowflakes

# Snowflake Maze

Start

End

# Trace over the letter outlines to complete the words.

TIGER

KITTEN

PANDA

LLAMA

Each snowflake has one match.
Color the matching pairs the same color!

# Trace the princess crown and then color it in.

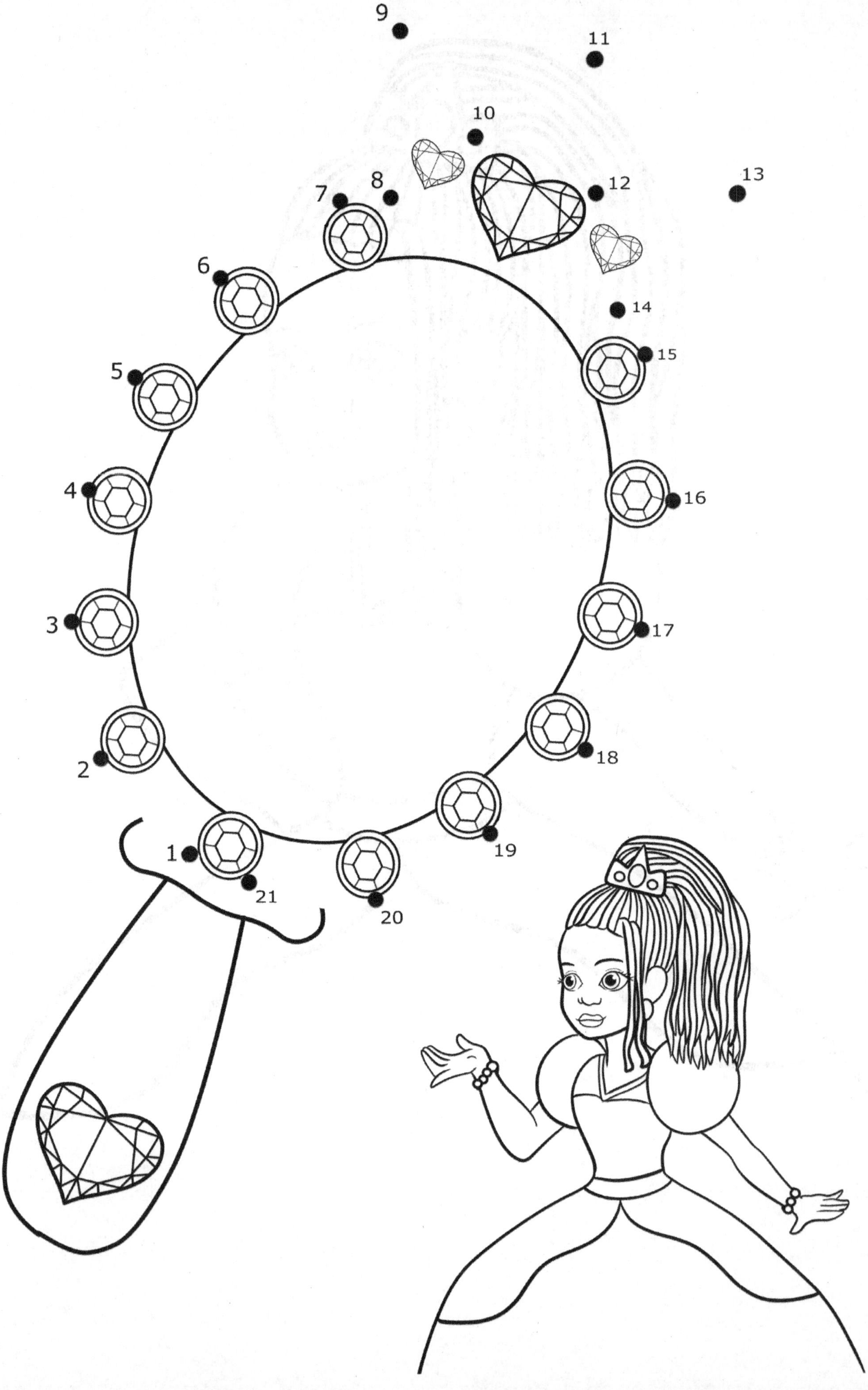

1
2
3
4
5
6
7
8
9
10
11
12
13
14
15
16
17
18
19
20
21

# Color by Number!
## 1 - Pink　　2 - Yellow　　3 - Purple
## 4 - Blue　　5 - Red

# Help the fish swim free from the maze.

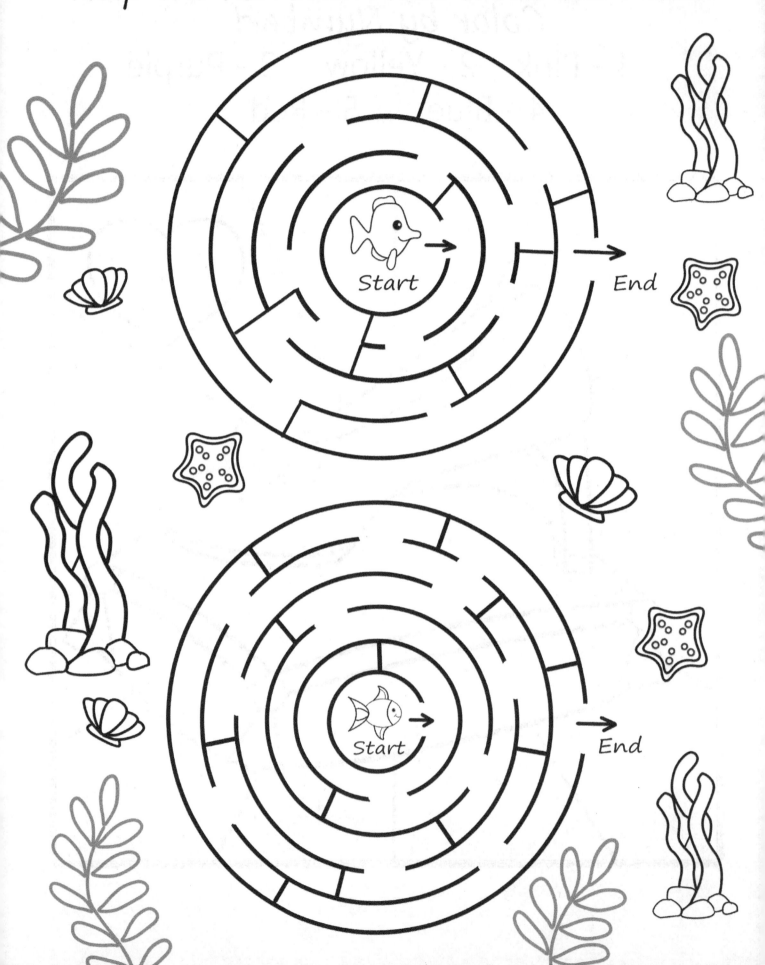

Start

End

Start

End

# Mermaid Word Search

```
M U D O L P H I N F
E T U R T L E U A Y
R C S E A S T A R Z
M K H L W O Q V W K
A G E F I S H M H E
I M L R F Z N O A L
D A L W L M Y I L P
W Z B U B B L E S M
```

## Search for and circle the hidden words!

 NARWHAL

 MERMAID

 FISH

 SHELL

 DOLPHIN

 SEASTAR

 BUBBLES

 KELP

 TURTLE

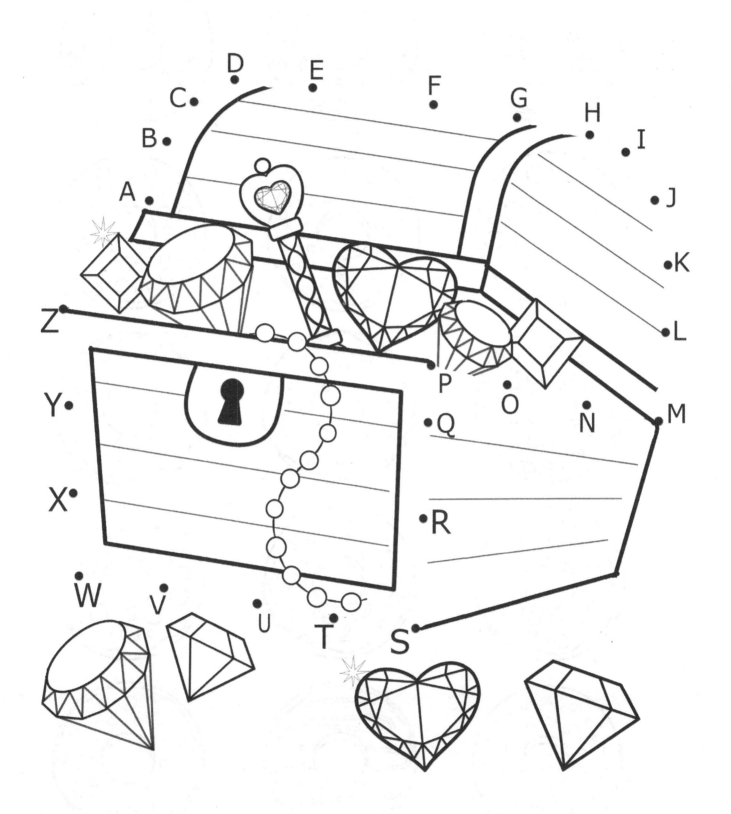

# Find and circle the donut that does NOT have a match

# Match the cupcake to its identical pair

# Color by Number!
1 - Pink   2 - Yellow   3 - Orange
4 - Blue   5 - Red

Help the tiger get to her ice cream.

Start

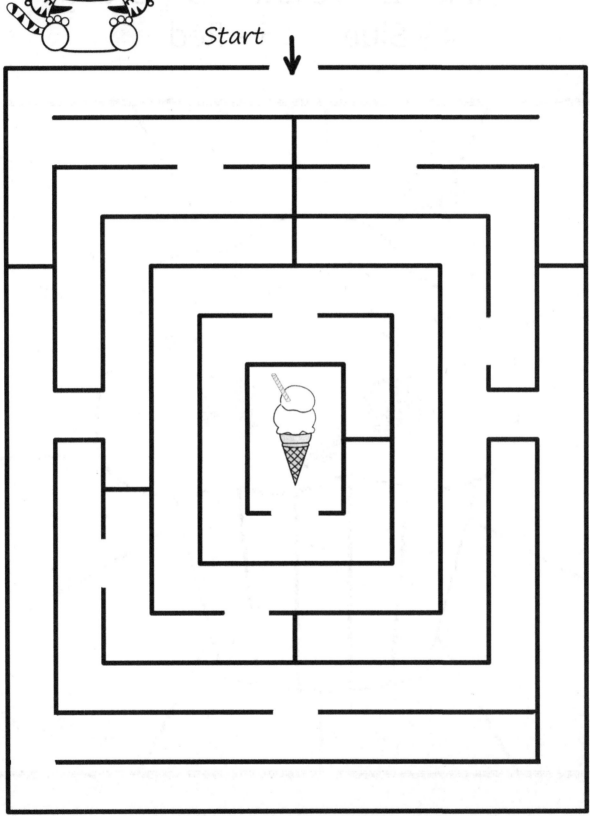

Can you trace the patterns on these turtle shells? Then, color them in!

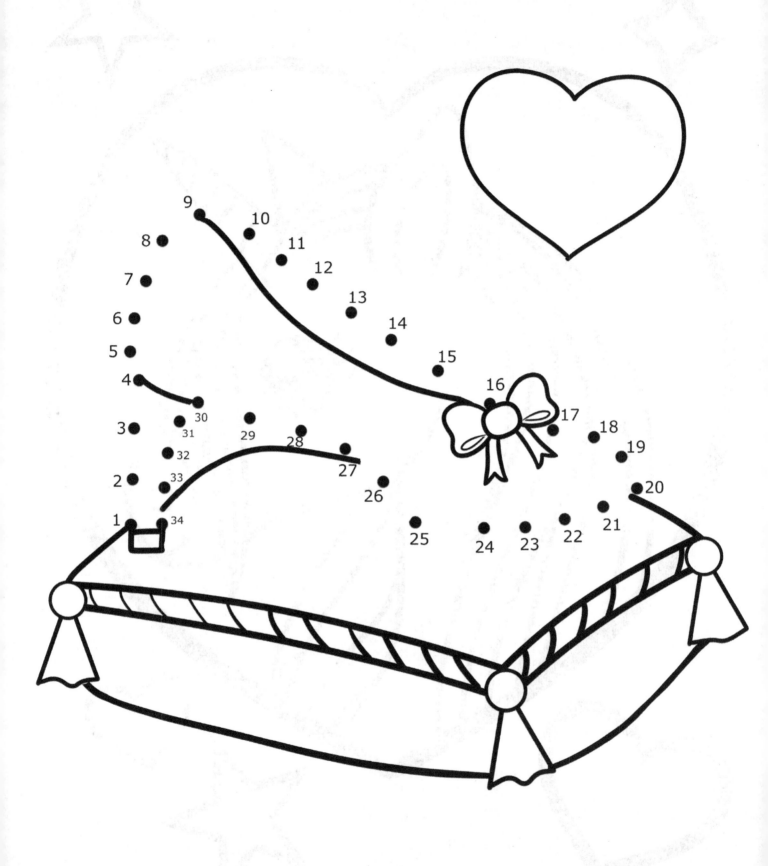

# Help the fairy fly out of the maze and into the flower garden!

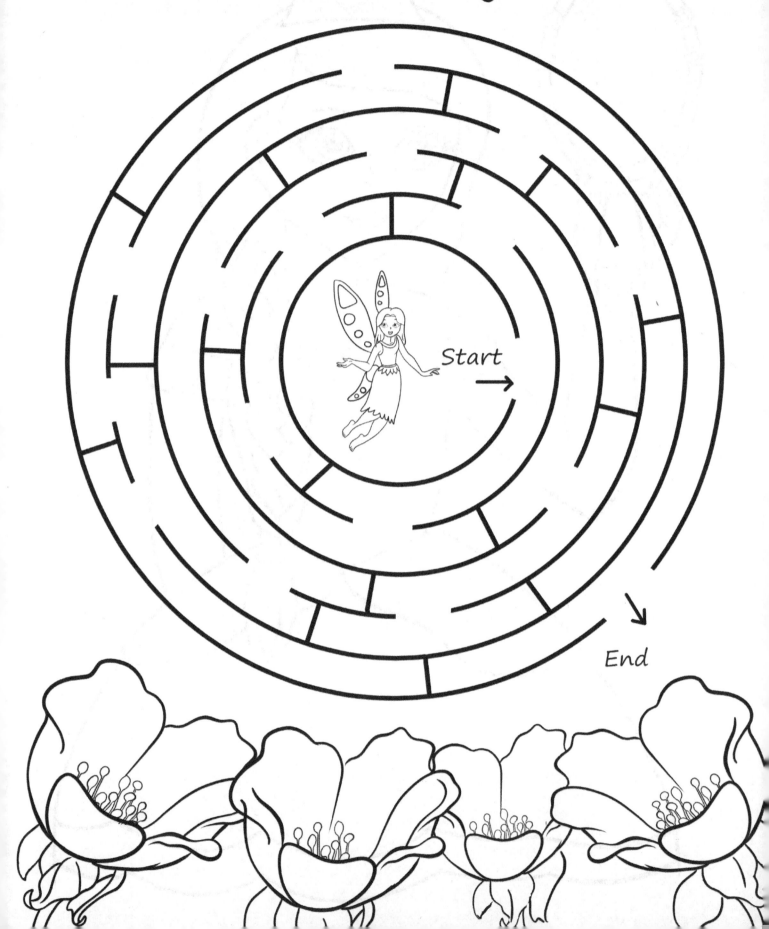

Start

End

One item in each row is different from the others.
Find and circle it!

Who is holding which balloon? Color the BUNNY'S ballon PINK.
Color the PENGUIN'S balloon RED. Color the TURTLE'S balloon PURPLE.

# Princess Dress Maze

Start

End

# Trace the shapes on the kites.

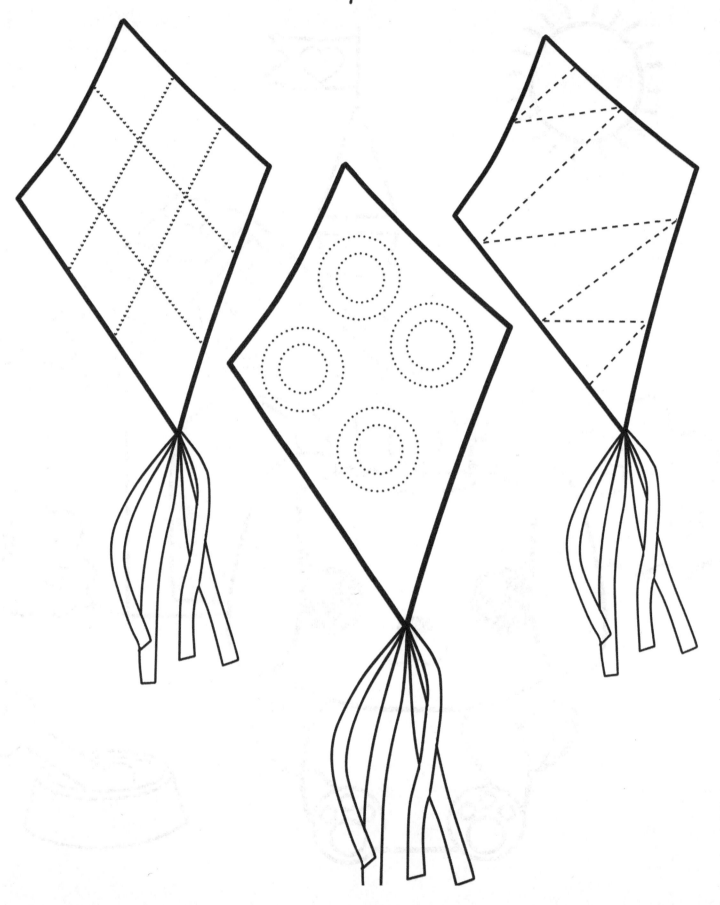

# Cupcake Maze

# Help the unicorn get to the rainbow!

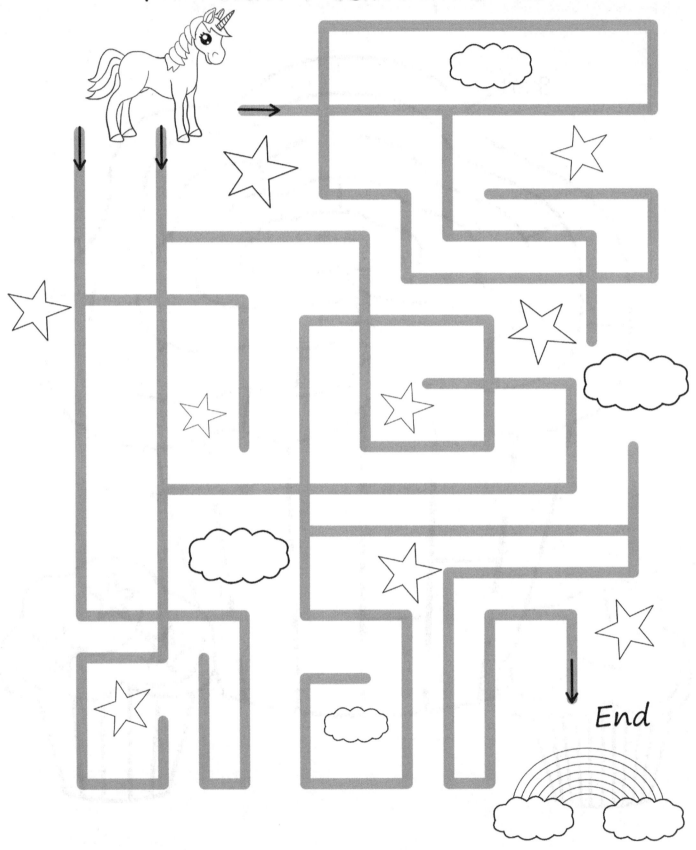

End

# Help the pegasus travel through the rainbow to reach the castle in the clouds.

Start

End

# I Spy! Find and count these objects

Did you find all of these?

# Princess Word Search

```
R I N G H S L P A E
U B H C A S T L E Y
N C D M N S H O E B
I R A L W O B V K R
C O X F B G E M A U
O W V R F Z N O P S
R N B W L M Y I B H
N Z P R I N C E S S
```

## Search for and circle the hidden words!

 RING     PRINCESS     SHOE

 CROWN     GEM     BRUSH

 UNICORN     CASTLE

Help all the animals take the right
paths to get to the cake in the middle.

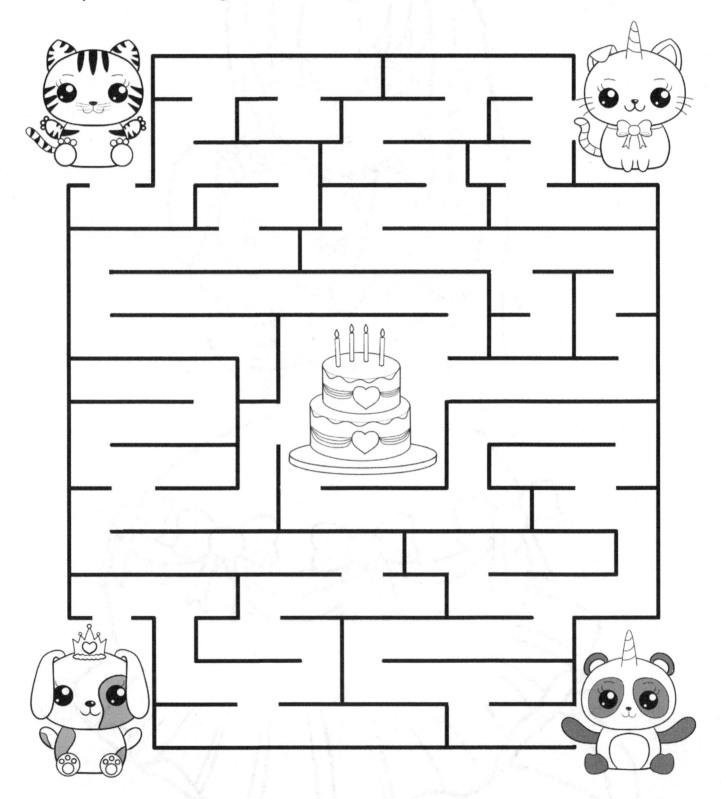

Count the spots on the ladybugs.
Then draw a line to the matching number.
Trace the numbers.

# Color by Number!

1 - Pink    2 - Yellow    3 - Orange
4 - Blue   5 - Red   6 - Brown  7- Purple

# Follow the trails. Which animal is flying which kite?

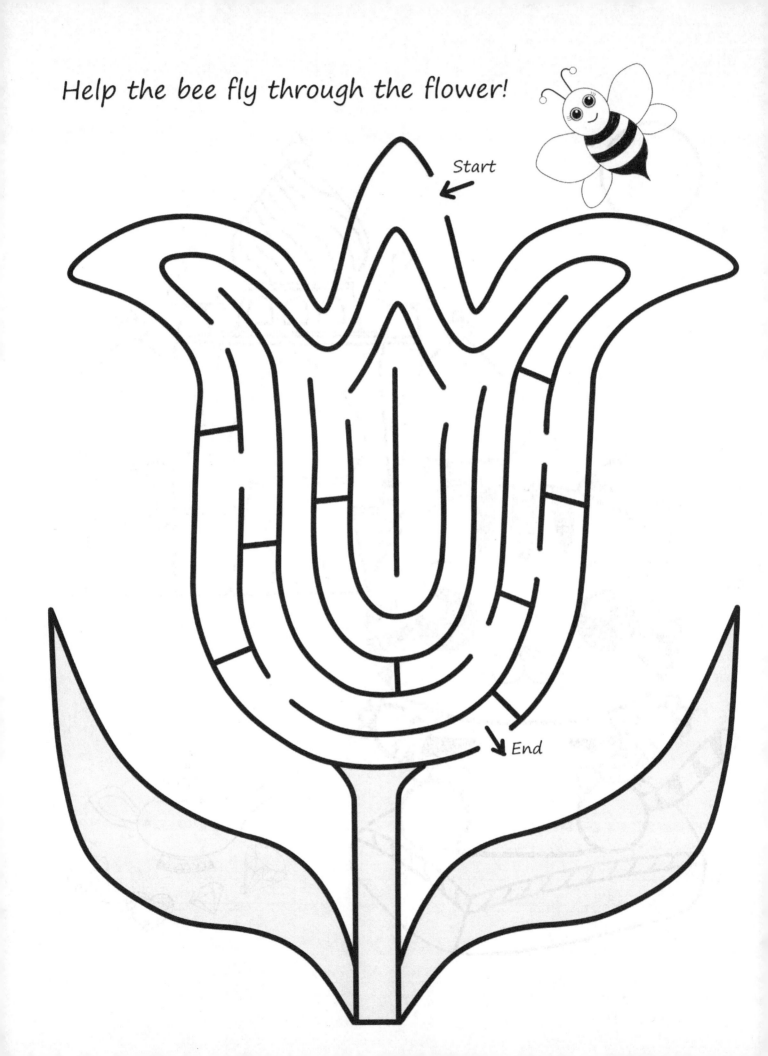

Help the bee fly through the flower!

Start

End

Color the butterflies and decorate them with your own patterns.

# Color the spaces the following colors:
**B** – Blue  **R** – Red
**Y** – Yellow  **P** – Pink

# Can you spot 7 differences between these pictures?

Color the heart shaped cake PINK, the recantangular shaped cake ORANGE, the circle shaped cake YELLOW and the star shaped cake PURPLE.

# Butterfly Maze

Start

End

# Princess Crown Maze

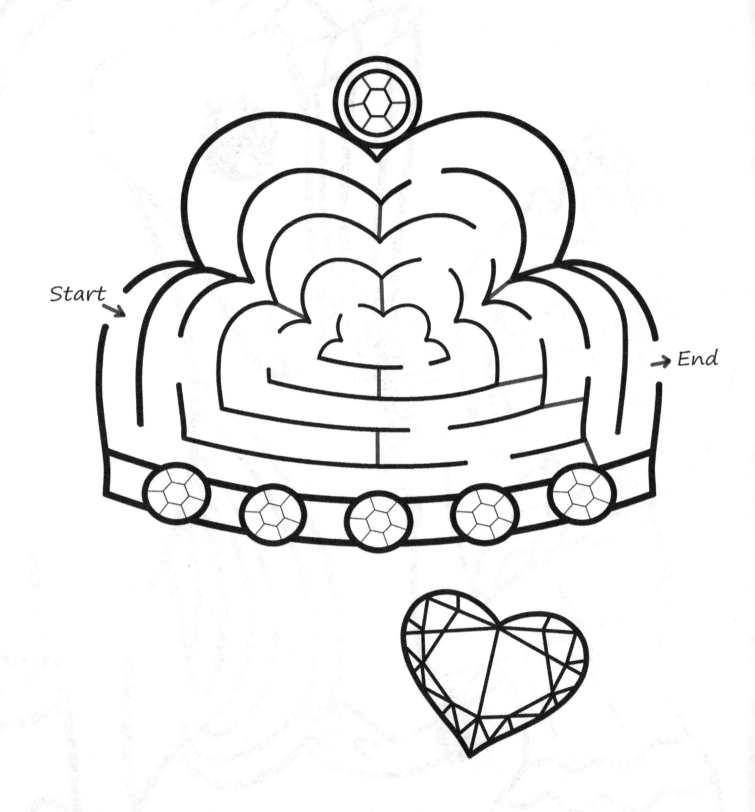

The princess is on her way to a party. Help her get to the castle and pick up three things along the way.

# Help the puppy get to her doghouse!

# Draw spots on the ladybugs,
## then color them in!
## How many ladybugs can you count?

Start

End

# Ice Cream Cone Maze

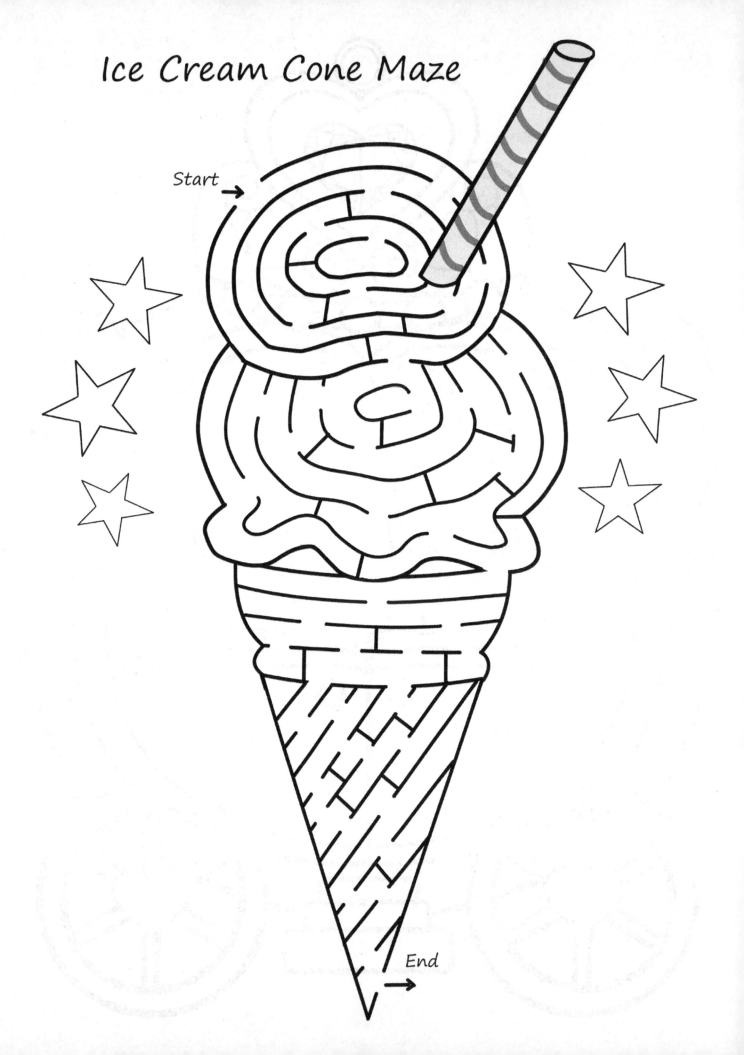

Start

End

# Color By Number!

1 - Red     2 - Orange     3 - Yellow

4 - Pink     5 - Blue     6 - Purple

# Help the bee fly to the center of the flower.

# Can you spot 8 differences between these pictures?

# I Spy! Find and count these objects

Did you find all of these?

# Follow the lines. Which path should the turtle take to get to the ladybug?

# Can you spot 8 differences between these pictures?

Color the CIRCLE shaped lollipop RED
Color the HEART shaped lollipop PINK
Color the STAR shaped lollipop YELLOW

# Fairy Word Search

| M | I | B | E | E | Z | L | P | L | E |
|---|---|---|---|---|---|---|---|---|---|
| U | B | H | C | U | S | T | Y | A | G |
| S | T | U | R | T | L | E | S | D | B |
| H | R | A | L | W | H | B | N | Y | S |
| R | O | S | E | B | I | E | A | B | U |
| O | W | V | R | F | L | N | I | U | N |
| O | N | B | W | L | M | Y | L | G | H |
| M | Z | F | A | I | R | Y | E | H | S |

## Search for and circle the hidden words!

 FAIRY

 BEE

 SNAIL

 ROSE

 LADYBUG

 SUN

 MUSHROOM

 TURTLE

# Draw a picture of yourself as a princess.

# Make Your Own Memory Matching Game

Color as many pictures as you like. Then, have an adult help you cut out the square cards. To play, use as many pairs of cards as you like. For younger children use fewer cards. Mix the cards and place them face down on a table. Players take turns turning over two cards. If they match the player keeps them. If the pictures are different they are placed back face down in the same spot. Play continues until all the picture cards are matched. The player with the most matches at the end wins.

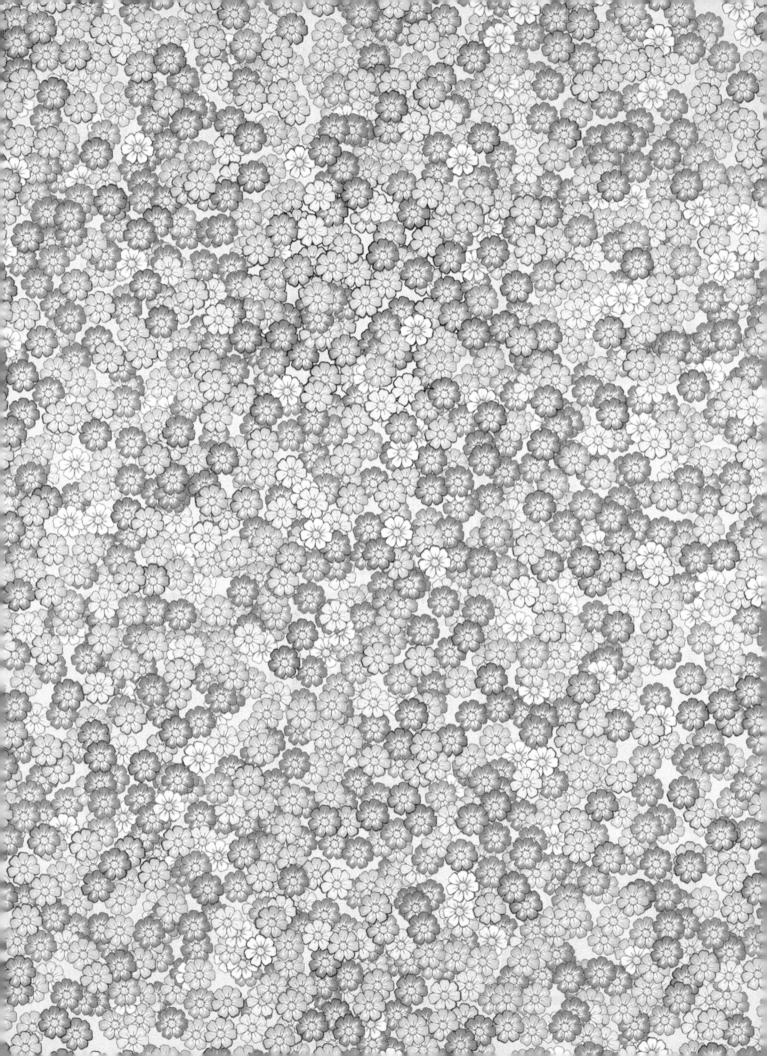

TURTLE

MERMAID

NARWHAL

TURTLE

MERMAID

NARWHAL

DOLPHIN

CROWN

SHOE

DOLPHIN

CROWN

SHOE

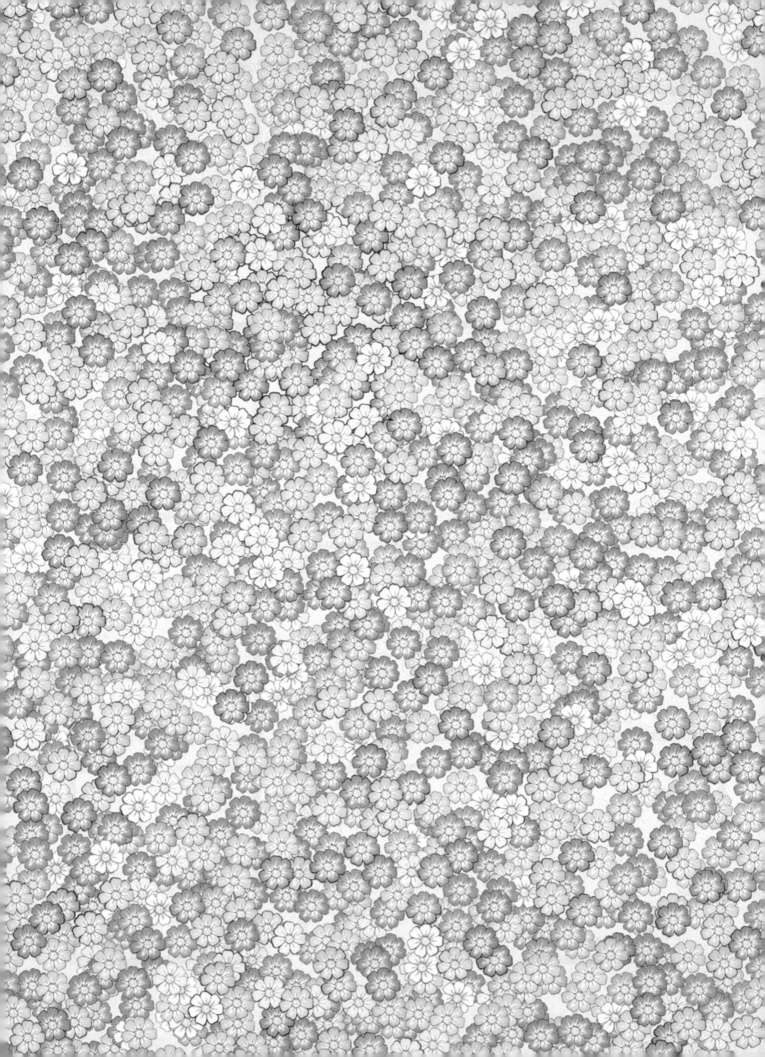

JELLYFISH

LADYBUG

PENGUIN

JELLYFISH

LADYBUG

PENGUIN

CUPCAKE

TIGER

RABBIT

CUPCAKE

TIGER

RABBIT

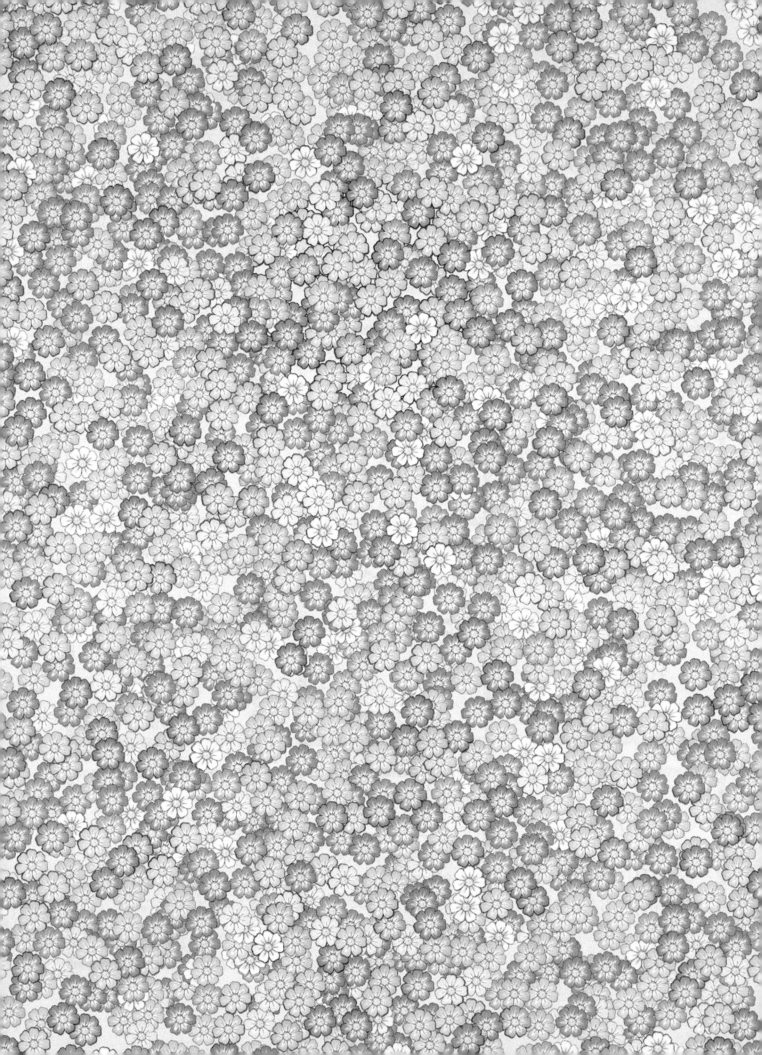